RTH-SOUTH PAPERBACK

Critical praise for

Meet the Molesons

rt vignettes introduce a thoroughly modern family of moles. Although their activities appear ordinary enough . . . the Molesons' experiences are never mundane. Bos's wry text features a casual, almost conversational tone. . . . Colorful illustrations add to the fun, depicting every foible of this quirky family. A refreshing reminder that easy readers can be both literary and interesting, this should appeal to beginning readers and their parents." *Booklist*

Meet the
Molesons

Stories by **Burny Bos**
Pictures by **Hans de Beer**

Translated by J. Alison James

North-South Books / New York

First published in the United States, Great Britain, Canada,
Australia, and New Zealand in 1994 by North-South Books,
an imprint of Nord-Süd Verlag AG, Gossau Zürich, Switzerland.
First paperback edition published in 1995.

Distributed in the United States by North-South Books Inc., New York.

Library of Congress Cataloging-in-Publication Data
Bos, Burny, 1944-
[Familie Maulwurf, bitte recht freundlich! English]
Meet the Molesons / stories by Burny Bos ; pictures by
Hans de Beer ; translated by J. Alison James.
Summary: Members of the Moleson family exchange birthday
presents, have a bike race, go camping, and enjoy other adventures.
[1. Family life—Fiction.] I. De Beer, Hans, ill. II. Title.
PZ7.B648498Me 1994
[Fic] — dc20 93-49587

ISBN 1-55858-257-6 (TRADE BINDING)
1 3 5 7 9 TB 10 8 6 4 2
ISBN 1-55858-258-4 (LIBRARY BINDING)
1 3 5 7 9 LB 10 8 6 4 2
ISBN 1-55858-409-9 (PAPERBACK)
1 3 5 7 9 PB 10 8 6 4 2

A CIP catalogue record for this book is available
from The British Library.

Printed in Belgium

Contents

Meet the Molesons

So you want to
meet my family?
Here we are.
That's my mother.
Her name is Molly.
She works at the
office. She is very busy. She is also very
funny.
My father's name is Morris. But
everybody calls him
Mud. He used to
work in the mines.
Now he runs around
the house all day.
He cooks. He
cleans. He orders us
around. Basically
he is okay.

My grandma is a little wild. She uses a
wheelchair. It is electric. It can go fast.
Very fast.
Then there is my sister. Dusty. Dusty and
I are twins. She was born four and a half
minutes before me. She will never let me
forget this as long as we live.
And then there's me. My name is Dug.
Short for Dugless.
I like to eat. I like
to sleep. I like to
play. You see, we
are a pretty
normal family.

Birthday Presents

Let me tell you about our last birthday party.

We woke up early—we always do on days when we get presents.

The house was dead silent. So we stayed in bed. You see, our parents like to surprise us on our birthday.

After a while, we heard them tiptoeing around the house. We heard a thump.

"They're hanging the decorations," Dusty said.

Wheeeee went the kettle. "They're making us hot chocolate," I said.

"I hope we get great presents," Dusty said.

"Shush," I whispered.
"Pretend to be asleep.
They're coming!"
"Happy birthday!"
they yelled.
We sat up and tried
to look surprised.
"Holy moley," Dusty
cried. "It's our
birthday!"

Mother handed Dusty a huge package.
Inside was a crane. A bright red crane
with working gears. Dusty was thrilled,
sort of.

Then they gave me a doll.
Can you believe that? A doll! With extra
clothes to dress her up.
I tried to grin. "Thanks a lot!" I said
brightly.
Mother smiled at Father. It was an
"I told you so" look.

Dusty and I played with our toys. Dusty
tried to hook her crane to a fire truck.
"You can't do that," I said. "That crane is
much too small to lift a whole truck."
I made my doll walk up the side of the
sofa. "Look, Dusty!" I said. "She's a
mountain climber."
"She would never climb a mountain in
those clothes!" Dusty said, and she
grabbed my new doll away.

"Fine," I said, and I took her crane. I did some real earth moving. Dusty changed my doll's clothes.

We heard Mother outside the door.

"Quick!" Dusty said. She gave the doll back and took the crane.

Mother looked in. "Do you like your presents?" she asked.

"Yes, Mother," we said sweetly.

Cheese!

Want to hear about the time Father took
a family picture?
A picture of the family had to have
Father in it too. But if he was in it, how
could he take the picture?
There's a special button on the camera.
When you push the button, the camera
goes *beep beep beep* for ten seconds before
it goes CLICK!

Father had ten seconds to get into
the picture.
Father looked through the camera.
"Children, come here now!" Mother said.
"Grandma, you get in the middle."
Dusty pushed in front of me. So I pushed
her back.
"Dug, stop bothering your sister!" Mother
said. "Stand up straight!"
Father was still looking through the
camera.
He was taking a long time.
"Hurry up and take the picture, Mud!"
Mother sounded angry.
"Okey-dokey. Get ready to say 'Cheese!'"
He pushed the button. "Here comes
the little birdie!" he cried.
Beep beep beep went the camera.
Father started running.
But just then . . .

CLICK

there came a real birdie. It was a pigeon.
And he needed to go. So he went.
SPLAT!
Father tried to duck. He stumbled.
He bumped into Mother. Mother bumped
into me. I bumped into Dusty.
Grandma took off.
CLICK! went the camera.
Mother looked at her family, lying on the
ground.

She laughed and laughed. Then she
stopped laughing. She had just noticed
that there were pigeon droppings on her
new blouse! She did not think that was
very funny.
"Yuck!" squealed
Dusty.
"Cool!" I said.
"It had just better
wash out!" Mother
said.

The Sick Day

One morning Dusty and I were getting
ready for school. I found Mother's red
lipstick in the bathroom.
I opened it up. It made red dots on my
face. I put on some more. Great!
Dusty noticed. "You look like you have
chicken pox."
"Oooh," I said. "I don't feel well. I think
I have to stay home from school."
"Give me that!" Dusty took the lipstick.
Soon we both had "chicken pox."

We went back to bed.

"Time for school!" Father called.

"Oooh!" we moaned.

Father ran in. "What's wrong?" he cried.

"We are sick," I said in a weak voice.

"We can't go to school," Dusty said.

Father nodded. "You are right," he said.

"It looks like a bad case of chicken pox.
You will have to stay in bed."

Father looked worried. "I am afraid it
will be boring for you," he said.

Father brought us
cakes, mint tea,
and books.
We were very happy.
I purred like a cat.
"This is heaven,"
Dusty said. "I
have never felt so
good being sick!"

But when Mother came home after work,
she called for us. This is it, we thought.
Now we're in trouble!
Mother said, "Where are the children?
Are they still at school?"
We heard Father tell her how sick we
were—with chicken pox.
"They weren't sick last night," Mother
said, surprised.
"She knows," whispered Dusty.
"Should we hide?" I asked.

We heard Mother come up the stairs.
We hid under the covers.
She went into the bathroom.
"Where's the lipstick?" Dusty whispered.
"You had it!" I said.
"No I didn't, you did."
This might have gone on for a long time,
but then we heard Mother's voice.
"Chicken pox? Ridiculous!" she said.
Now we were really worried.

In a few minutes, Mother came into our
room. She looked terrible. She was
covered with red spots.

"Oh, oh, oh!" she moaned.

Father came running up the stairs. "Are
you sick too?" he asked. "I'll make you
some tea. Just lie down and rest."

Mother snuggled into bed with us and
said, "What a good man he is."

The Bicycle Race

One morning Mother and Father were
having an argument. Mother said Father
was too fat. She said he needed exercise.
Father said Mother needed exercise too.
Finally they decided to go on a family
bicycle ride.
Dusty rode behind Mother. I rode behind
Father. He turned and grinned at me.
"Let's find out just who needs exercise."
He took off like the wind.

"Watch out!" Mother called.

"What?" Father looked back to see what she wanted.

"Slow down!" Mother cried.

"I'll show her," Father mumbled, and he leaned down and pumped his legs faster and faster, until . . . CRASH!

The bike ran right into a tree.

Father and I flipped through the air and landed hard on the ground.

I had the breath knocked out of me.
The bike was up in the tree.
Father sat up and looked at me. "Are you
hurt?" he asked.
I nodded, even though I wasn't really
hurt.
Mother pulled up then, and said in her
cold voice, "Come on, Dug dear. Climb
up behind Dusty and I'll take you home."

"Does he have to?" Dusty whined.

"You two sit still," Mother said. She was not happy.

"What about me?" asked Father.

"You can walk," Mother said.

She turned her bike around and rode off with us. We went slowly.

"What about Father?" Dusty asked.

"I'll pick him up with the car later," Mother said. Then she explained, "I just can't stand it when he tries to show off."

I turned around for one last look.
Father looked up at his bike. He stamped
his foot in anger.
The tree trembled, and the bike fell
down. Right on his head.
I tried not to laugh.

Happy Campers

Father decided that we would go
camping one weekend.
"Hurrah!" Dusty and I shouted. We had a
brand-new tent to sleep in.
"Do you think you should try setting up
the tent once before we go?" Mother asked.
"Nah," said Father. "I read the
instructions. It's as easy as pie!"
"What kind of pie?" Mother asked. But
Father didn't seem to hear.
Late that afternoon, we drove to the
campsite.

Father stomped around like a general.
"All right, Dusty. You hold the pole in
that corner. Dug, you come here and
hold your pole. And don't fidget!"
He shook out the tent and searched for
the tent pegs. "I know I brought them,"
he mumbled.
"My arms are tired," Dusty whined.
Mother had supper cooking on the fire.
"Isn't that thing set up yet?" she asked.
"It's taking hours."
"You could help," Father grumbled.

Right after supper it started to rain.
Father ran to open the tent, but the zipper
was stuck. He pulled and tugged. He
pulled so hard that the tent fell down!
Now the rain was a storm.
Mother shook her head.
"Come on, let's find someplace dry."

She took off toward the toilets.
At first Dusty and I didn't want to go.
We wanted to sleep in the tent.
But the rain was cold, and we were tired.
At last we went to find Mother.
Father stayed outside.
He would not give up.

Mother had made us each a warm little bed. We fell fast asleep.

We didn't hear Father when he came in. We didn't hear him tell us we could come and sleep in the tent now. We didn't hear him say, "Fine. I'll sleep in it myself!"

We just kept on sleeping.

So Father took his sleeping bag and went back to the tent.

In the morning, Mother was grumpy. Her
back was sore from sleeping on the floor.
Father was happy. "Isn't it a wonderful
tent?" he said. "I always sleep so well in
the great outdoors!"

Grandma's Speeding Ticket

Grandma was driving
her electric wheelchair
down the street.
We ran outside.
"Wait for us,
Grandma!" Dusty
called. We tried to catch up.
"I'm faster than you are," Grandma
called happily.
Father was watching through the
window.
"Slow down or you'll break your neck!"
he called.
Grandma put on the brakes.
Dusty and I skidded to a stop.
"Do you two want a ride?" Grandma
asked.
"You bet!" I said.
"Is that allowed?" Dusty asked.

"Of course it is," Grandma said. "It is my wheelchair!"
We took off.
The three of us roared down the street.
Dusty squealed. I held on to my hat.
"Fast, isn't it?" Grandma said proudly.
A young police officer on a motorcycle saw us speeding by.

"What do you think you're doing?" he
asked. "I'm sure it must be against the
law to give wheelchair rides."
Grandma said, "But Dug and Dusty are
my grandchildren!" Why did she have
to say our names? We almost died.

"Nice kids," said the police officer. "But that doesn't change the law. Next time I'll have to give you a fine."
Father had seen everything. He thought the policeman was giving Grandma a ticket. That made him angry.

Father came running.

"It's all right, Mud," Grandma said.

Father did not listen. He yelled at the policeman: "What do you think you're doing, giving a ticket to an elderly woman, you clown . . ."

"But nothing happened, Father," Dusty said. I tried to hold Father back, but he was too far gone.

The police officer pulled out his little book and wrote Father a ticket.

Sometimes my father is pretty stupid.

The Christmas Train

Christmas finally came. We got the
greatest present: more track and a new
engine for our electric train.
Mother said, "Santa certainly got it right
this year!"
Father looked as proud as if he had
thought of it himself.

Then I got a wonderful idea. I whispered
it into Dusty's ear. She grinned.
"We have a Christmas surprise for you.
But you have to get dressed up for it."
"That sounds like fun," Mother said.
"I can't wait," Father said.
They went obediently up to their
bedroom.
Dusty and I went to work.

We laid the track all the way from the
living room into the kitchen. Then we
went to the kitchen and loaded up the
train with chunks of cheese and nuts.
Dusty poured four glasses of juice.
Carefully she set them on a freight car.
Mother and Father came down the stairs
at just the right time.
"Close your eyes!" called Dusty.
She led them both to the sofa.

When they were sitting down, she gave
me the sign and I flipped the switch.
"Now look!" Dusty cried.
The train drove in. I slowed it down
and brought it to a stop right in front of
the sofa.
Mother and Father clapped their hands.
"What a nice surprise!" Mother said.
"Brilliant!" Father said. He straightened
his tie. "Such a good idea, it could have
been one of mine."
Everyone laughed.

"I don't see what is so funny," Father
said, and he handed out the glasses
of juice.
Everyone laughed again.
"This is really a delicious Christmas
train, isn't it, darling?" Mother said,
and she gave Father a big kiss.

I could tell you a million other stories about my family—like the time that Father was painting and Grandma zoomed into his ladder . . . or the time that Dusty got lost in a pickle factory and I had to find her . . . or the time some ants ate our picnic lunch . . . but right now it's time for dinner, and I've got to go. So good-bye, for now.

About the Author

Burny Bos was born in Haarlem, Holland. He began his career as a teacher and in 1973 he started developing children's programs for Dutch radio. Within a few years he was working for Dutch television as well. He currently makes records and cassette tapes for children and has won many prizes for his children's broadcasts, films, and recordings. He has also written more than 25 children's books, several of which have been illustrated by Hans de Beer.

He lives with his wife, two daughters, and a little son in Bussum, which is near Amsterdam.

ABOUT THE ILLUSTRATOR

Hans de Beer was born in 1957 in Muiden, a small town near Amsterdam, in Holland. He began to draw when he went to school, mostly when the lessons got too boring. In college he studied history, but he was drawing so many pictures during the lectures that he decided to become an artist. He went on to study illustration at the Rietveld Academy of Art in Amsterdam.

Hans de Beer's first book, *Little Polar Bear*, was very popular around the world. The book has been published in 18 languages. Hans had so much fun illustrating picture books that he did more and more of them. He likes to draw polar bears, cats, walruses, elephants, and moles.

His books have received many prizes, among them the first prize from an international jury of children in Bologna, Italy.

Hans de Beer now lives in Amsterdam with his wife, who is also a children's book illustrator.

Mia the Beach Cat
by Wolfram Hänel, illustrated by Kirsten Höecker

The Old Man and the Bear
by Wolfram Hänel, illustrated by Jean-Pierre Corderoc'h

Lila's Little Dinosaur
by Wolfram Hänel, illustrated by Alex de Wolf

Meet the Molesons
by Burny Bos, illustrated by Hans de Beer